Stories

D0814476

from

Real
Life

Stories

from

Real
Life

*— with love,
as always
T. C.*

*peter
wilm*

Tony Crunk

art by Peter Wilm

*♡ U, weena!
☺*

GreencupBooks

Library of Congress Cataloging-in-Publication Data
available from the Library of Congress
ISBN-10: 0-9786615-4-0
ISBN-13: 978-0-9786615-4-0

Text design by Russell Helms
Cover design by Russell Helms

Cover art (screened) by Peter Wilm;
all interior art by Peter Wilm

Available at fine book stores, Amazon.com, and directly
from the publisher:

GreencupBooks
P.O. Box 660260
Vestavia Hills, AL 35266
www.greencupbooks.com

Contents

Big Hands

Yes. You could say they were big. You could say, in fact, they were very big. And the worst of it was, they got bigger.

Whenever he was nervous or self-conscious, his hands would grow bigger. And bigger. Until they were the size of beach balls. Or even bigger.

So he could never sit in a dentist's lobby or wait for a job interview without tearing the pages of the magazine he was reading or knocking over the potted rubber tree in the corner with his hands, his big hands.

And once, when he was in high school, he was on a date with a girl. She was a very beautiful girl. They were at a movie. It was a Chuck Norris movie.

And he was wondering whether he should try to put his arm around her, and of course as soon as he wonders this, his hands start growing bigger. And they grow bigger, and even bigger, until they're about the size of portable TV sets.

"I'll be back in a minute," he whispers, and sets his 7-up down on the floor, and of course he spills it, and he hands her the box of popcorn they've been sharing, and of course he spills popcorn in her lap. And he goes up to the restroom to run some cold water over his hands, his big hands, thinking that that might shrink them back down again.

But he can't even get his hands under the faucet, they're so big by now. And of course water splashes out all over him. And of course now he can't go back out of the restroom because he's got water spots all over the front of him and it'll look like he pissed his pants.

So there's nothing to do of course but go sit in one of the stalls and wait for his pants to dry.

So he's sitting there. And he's sitting there. And then of course into the restroom comes some kid with his father. And the kid is not at all well behaved. The kid, in fact, is tearing around the restroom like something just that minute let out of hell.

So of course the guy with the big hands sitting in the stall looks down and sees this kid's face looking up at him from under the stall door. And of course the kid jumps up and hollers, "Daddy Daddy. There's a man sitting in there with his pants still on."

And of course the father asks him, "What?" And the kid repeats it, and of course the father says something under his breath about all the weird-ohs out in public these days and about going to get the manager.

And of course the guy's hands by this time are the size of one of the minor planets and he can't even get the stall door unlatched. And so of course here comes the man and his kid and this time they've got the manager, and of course the manager is standing there banging on the stall door saying, "Hey! what's going on in there?"

So by the time the guy with the big hands explains everything to the manager and calms down enough for his hands to return to normal, he walks out of the restroom just in time to see this girl, this very beautiful girl, out in front of the theatre climbing into the car with her father, whom she's called to come get her—the movie's over, the lobby is empty, the woman in the ticket booth is counting the cash, and all you can hear is the hum of the fluorescent light inside the popcorn machine. . .

4

And now, tonight, this guy is older. And his life has begun to look the same way it will look five years from now. Maybe even ten years from now.

And tonight he's had to leave a party because he was standing in the kitchen trying to open a beer and his hands, his big hands, knocked the Cuisinart off into the sink, cracking a colander.

So now, now he's walking down the damp street, in and out of the circles of light from the street lamps, and he's pulling his collar up around his neck, and he knows, he knows, what they're doing now, back there at the party— they're all sitting around the living room, listening to bad jazz, smoking some cheap green pot that somebody grew in their basement, saying, "Hey! Who was that guy with those big hands?"

Smoking

My greatest fear is the fear of looking up and finding my-self the best-dressed person in a bus station.

Because in a bus station everyone is going about their business and someone is pulling a handle on a vending machine and someone is opening a shopping bag and one of the drivers is walking by popping gum and someone is leading a kid into the restroom and then the clock ticks and everyone is standing still like in a photograph and a soldier is asleep in front of a coin-op TV and a man by the ticket counter in corduroy pants looks like my father and the route map on the wall is a huge bloodshot eye and the clock ticks and there is motion and the clock ticks and there is inertia and the clock ticks and you are now here and the clock ticks and, buddy, you are nowhere.

So that's why I took up smoking.

Because if you smoke you can walk up to some guy leaning in the doorway of the snack bar and say, "Got a light?"

And he can say, "Sure," or maybe say nothing, just hand you some matches.

And you can light one up and blow out some smoke and say, "Where you headed?"

And he can light one up too and say, "Smyrna," but not say whether it's Smyrna, Tennessee or Smyrna, Georgia, and anyway it's probably a lie, so it doesn't matter, because you can take another puff and blow out some more smoke and say, "Yeah? I got a sister lives in Smyrna."

The Bedouins

A tribe of wandering Bedouins made camp late one afternoon in Robert and Martha's backyard.

"Robert," said Martha, peeking through the Venetian blinds in the kitchen. "Did you see these Bedouins in the backyard?"

"What the hell. . . ?" said Robert, who had just gotten home from work. "Well damned if it ain't," he said, joining Martha at the window. "By god, I won't have it. I've a good mind to go out there right now and run the whole lot of them off."

"I wonder if they'd like some lemonade," said Martha. She went out with a pitcher and some tumblers on a tray and asked the Bedouins if they'd like some nice cold lemonade. Fresh.

The Bedouins thought she'd asked to see an exhibition of traditional Bedouin folk dances. So they dropped their preparations for making camp, left tents and rugs and camels and goats and baskets spread out across the lawn, put on colorful native costumes and did a whirling sort of dance for her. With swords.

"Well, thank you," said Martha, when the Bedouins had finished. Then she went back inside to start supper. "Those Bedouins are so nice," she said to Robert.

But Robert mumbled about them all through supper. And during a commercial after supper, Martha went out into the kitchen and found him peeking through the blinds again. "By god," he said, "I've a good mind to call the sheriff over here and arrest the whole bunch of them. I'm not putting up with this, I tell you."

"I wonder if they'll be warm enough tonight," said Martha. She went out to see if the Bedouins needed some extra blankets.

The Bedouins thought she'd asked to hear an ancient Bedouin folk tale. So they told her one. It was about a princess and a white steed and a tiger. Martha sat with the Bedouins in a circle, gazing into the middle of the red fire, the stars sprinkled overhead like rhinestones on angels' dresses.

Martha didn't understand a word the Bedouins said. But when they finished with their story, she smiled very warmly and said, "Thank you. Thank you very much," and went back inside.

"I don't think they need any more blankets," she said to Robert. "Come on, honey. It's time for bed."

Late in the night, Martha came downstairs to turn the kitchen light off. Robert was standing by the window in his bathrobe. "By god, Martha," he whispered hoarsely. "I've got a good mind to get my twelve-gauge down and show them all a thing or two. I'm not putting up with this…"

Martha touched his arm. "Come on, honey," she said. "You need your rest."

The next morning, Robert came down to the kitchen in his pajamas, snapped the morning paper up off the table and poured some coffee.

"The Bedouins left a while ago," said Martha. "Just after sun-up. I made them some sandwiches and saw them off."

"Damn lucky for them they left before I got up," said Robert. "I'd had just about all of them Bedouins I was going to take."

Roger

That night, Roger cried himself to sleep.

"I can't go on," he sobbed into his pillow. "I can't go on. I can't go on."

The next day was Thursday. The sun rose. Roger got up, put on his pants, and went to work.

Giant Rodents
from Outer Space

They came from outer space. Hordes and hordes of giant rodents. Some of them as tall as buildings.

Their fur was slick and oily. Their rodent-like cry was horrible and piercing enough to shatter concrete. They smelled awful.

The giant rodents emerged from their giant, cigar-shaped spacecraft in every corner of the world and roamed the streets and countrysides, destroying everything, everything in their paths. Panic and terror raced like flame, unchecked, across the face of the globe.

My mother called me in the middle of the night, crying, hysterical, to tell me a couple of them were trying to get in through her bedroom window. She tends to kind of overreact to that sort of thing, you know?

The Acrobat

I worked at a liquor store once. It was in a bad neighborhood.

When you came in through the front door, you were standing inside a sort of cage of metal bars, behind which were the shelves of liquor and the checkout counter, which came up to about your shoulders. You would have to tell one of us what you wanted, and we would have to get it for you, and you would have to hand us your money through the bars and we would hand you your change and your bottle through the bars. It was in a bad neighborhood.

The circus came through one night and played at the Civic Center about two blocks away. They piped calliope music through outdoor loudspeakers all afternoon. You could hear it all over the neighborhood. It was August.

In the early evening, the regulars started gathering in the alley behind the store, where they spent every evening in the summer bumming nickels and dimes from each other and from other people to buy pints of wine, which they'd walk all over the neighborhood trying to hide from each other. The regulars had nothing.

But one of them had something. His name was Mackerel. Mackerel wore an old striped engineer's cap and he didn't have many teeth left and the story was he'd only recently gotten out of prison and the joke was that you could help Mackerel stay out of prison if you wouldn't bend over any time he came around and he had a portable transistor radio in a blue leather carrying case and he carried it with him, everywhere.

The night of the circus, late, when you could hear the streetlights in the parking lot humming above the noise of the traffic, which was winding down, Mackerel walked up to the store's drive-in window, more drunk even than usual, and set his transistor radio down, blaring, on the pavement beside him, and acted for every bit of fifteen minutes like an acrobat in the circus.

He even made the noises of the crowd cheering.

James, Who
Wrote Poetry

"My son James is such a sensitive boy," said James's mother to her friends at P.T.O. meetings. Regularly. "He writes poetry, you know."

James was in the eleventh grade. He had taken to reading Frost and walking through old graveyards. He felt sad about things and wrote poems about his experiences.

"Autumn is my favorite season," he wrote in his diary. "Leaves fall, and the grass turns brown, reminding me that all living things must wither away and die, just as in the spring they bloom and come to life. In autumn, I am sad and alone, but life is sad and lonely, and I am but a small part of life."

During this period, most of James's poems were about death.

James started to feel that his parents didn't understand him. And it was true. James's father couldn't understand why James didn't want to join the Masonic lodge, or why he didn't ask for a new CB radio for Christmas. James's mother couldn't understand why James didn't want to wear his new blue leisure suit to the prom.

When James went away to college, he took a course in Creative Writing. His instructor told him he should try to be a little less "didactic."

"Ah, yes. Didactic," said James, who then spent the weekend staring out his dorm window thinking about it and not shaving.

In college, James majored in English and started wearing an old army fatigue jacket. He took to reading Ginsberg and identifying with the seamier sides of life.

"My friends mean well," he wrote in his diary, which had now become his journal. "But they could never understand the true anguish of genuine alienation. Only the real outcasts of society understand this fully."

During this period, most of James's poems were about drunks who wore old shoes and street people who lived in shelters and flop houses. James had never been in a flop house, but once when he was a kid his father had taken him to a diner downtown that had a pool room in the back and had let James peek through the curtain at it.

James got some of his poems published in the college literary magazine. He felt he had come a long way.

"I was especially moved by the one about the old man in front of the Third Street Mission," said Glenda, another English major whom James wound up marrying.

After he graduated, James went to work in a factory that made plastic mouthwash bottles. Then he got fed up with that and went to business school for a while.

He got a job eventually as manager of a fish-and-chips place.

The Thing that Happened

Once upon a time there were some people.

And these people had words for everything that was and for everything that happened. And the people talked to each other using these words. "Tree," one of the people would say. "Yes, tree," another would say. "Tree falls," one of the people would say. "Yes, tree falls," another would say.

In this way the people could tell each other what was and what happened. It was a very clever system.

But then one day something happened, which the people did not have a word for. This was very disconcerting. Everybody knew what happened, since it had happened shortly before dinner, when everyone had just gotten in from hunting and gathering wild nuts and berries. But no one knew the word for it, so they couldn't talk about it.

And since they had no word for it, and therefore couldn't talk about it, everybody lurched off to their huts and just sort of sat around thinking about it.

A strange and fearful look came into their eyes. They sat up all night, peering out into the darkness, thinking about what had happened but which there was no word for.

They continued in this state for several dread-filled days. They became afraid to go out of their huts, afraid that something else might happen which there was no word for.

Finally, one of the more thoughtful among them said, "Enough is enough." So he made up a new word for the thing that had happened that nobody had had a word for.

That afternoon, he went out into the clearing between the huts and called all the people together, and they came and stood around him under the swaying binjo-binjo tree, and they listened, and he spoke.

"God," he said. And all the people sighed with great relief.

"God," they all said.

And they found that they could then talk about what had happened and could tell each other what had happened. A terrible black cloud was lifted from them.

So after that if anything happened that the people didn't have a word for, they all said, "God." If a tree fell for no apparent reason, or if a coffee cup broke, or if one night some twelve or thirteen of them sank with their tree-bark boat to the bottom of the black water while fishing beneath the bone-faced moon and the dripping net of stars, one of the people would say, "God," and another one of the people would say, "Yes, God," and there was no need for any further discussion.

How the Bearded Lady
Lost Her Husband

After work, he stopped by Red's and picked up a six, and took it to the park and sat in the shadows behind a statue of a guy with a crew cut blessing the Indians, and drank it, and watched night come.

When he got home, he walked in the door, took one look at her, and said, "Goddammit. You are so hairy. I hate looking at all that hair."

Then he went back out, climbed into his 1976 Grand Prix with the one wobbly fender, and drove all night to South Dakota.

Thunder

A great peal of thunder rolls out from grandmother's thimble on the table. We all gather around, hands folded solemnly in front of us.

Grandmother leans forward, raising her spectacles, and peers into the thimble.

We say, "Tell us, grandmother. What do you see?"

She says, "I see a forest. All the trees are black, with empty branches. It looks kind of like rain."

We notice for the first time that grandmother's skin has begun to look yellow, like old paper. "No, grandmother, no," we say. "It's only a thimble. Do not leave us."

"Hey. And there's some guy," she says, "wearing a red vest."

"No, grandmother. Please," we say. "We will love you always."

"Looks like he's selling something," she says. "Lapel pins or something. Maybe belt buckles..."

"Please. . .," we say again.

But grandmother is no longer with us.

Just her spectacles lying on the chair, her needle, still warm, lying by the flickering lamp.

The Girl and the Dog: A Romance

The snow was melting.

A girl walked, with her toes pointing slightly outward, along the broken concrete path of an old city park.

A big gray dog followed her. The dog's head came full up to the girl's waist, and she jumped when it first nudged her from behind.

The girl wore a big wool coat, its belt hanging down loose in the back.

She went and sat in a tire swing that hung by a rope from a tree. Then she went and leaned her head languidly against the ladder of the slide. The big gray dog watched her.

The girl left the park, and the big gray dog followed her.

She went up to a house. She opened the big wooden door with the big glass pane and the hand-turned bell that didn't work anymore.

The big dog followed her in, and the window rattled in the door when the girl shut it.

The big gray dog followed her up the stairs.

They came into a room that smelled like old upholstery. On a coffee table was a half-full glass of Coke with a layer of melted ice on top, a too-full ashtray, and a magazine opened to a gray page.

The girl shut the door behind them. Then she closed the red curtains at the tall window. That made it dark, but the late sunlight still filtered in through the yellowed fringe lace and lit up the dust in the air.

The girl sat down on the couch, which had one bent leg. The stuffings showed through the threadbare arms.

She looked at the dog and said, "O.K., dog. You can leave now."

But the big gray dog did not leave. . .

The Kid with Two Fathers

One of them was Frank, who drove a dump truck at the quarry and had a tattoo on his leg that Jimmy wasn't supposed to stare at. The kid's name was Jimmy.

But Buddy Wright down the street said, "He's not your real father, he's just your mother's boyfriend living off the child support from your real father, who's a drunk and he lives over in Grayson County now, my sister said so."

Jimmy said, "Shut up Buddy Wright, he is so my father."

And Buddy Wright said, "You shut up you little punk, you don't know anything, I'll bet you don't even know what screwing is."

So Jimmy went home and sat on the back steps and ate some Froot Loops out of the box and watched some ants and didn't think much more about it.

But then a few nights soon after that Jimmy heard some whispering, so he snuck down the hall and watched Frank and his mother mess around naked in bed, so he went back to his room and lay awake and thought some more about what Buddy Wright had said.

Somewhere down the alley somebody's dog barked most of the night.

The next day was Sunday. When Jimmy came home from Sunday School Frank was lying on his back in the front yard under his dump truck. Jimmy walked up to his feet, which were sticking out and said, "You're not my real father."

Frank said, "Hell, boy, you don't know anything, go get me some pliers out of the garage."

Jimmy came back with the pliers and said, "You're not my real father, God is my real father, and he is in heaven, and he made me, because I asked Mrs. Marsten."

Frank hollered, "Goddamn gasket." So Jimmy went inside and turned on *Mutual of Omaha's Wild Kingdom* and didn't think much else about it.

After that, though, when Frank made Jimmy go to bed before *Battlestar Gallactica* or hollered at him to get out of that goddamn truck right this minute Jimmy would say, "You're not my real father, my real father sees everything you do, and I hate you." But usually he would just get hollered at some more for saying it, so usually he just said it to himself.

Jimmy's mother was named Carla. One day when Jimmy came home from Sunday School Carla was in the kitchen dropping potatoes into the pressure cooker. Steam was flying up around her face.

Jimmy climbed up on a chair and said, "I know Frank's not my real father, but I know where my real father is, and someday I'm going to go live with him."

Carla gave Jimmy a look and said, "Where'd you get that big idea, and I thought I told you once to throw that banana peel away didn't I?"

So Jimmy threw his banana peel away and went out into the driveway and tried to make a radar receiver out of some pop top rings and a piece of inner tube and didn't think much else about it.

But one day soon after that he came home from Sunday School and Frank was lying in bed in his underwear watching the game. Jimmy walked up to the bed and said, "When my big brother gets here he won't ever let you holler at me again."

Frank said, "Hell boy you don't know anything, you don't even have any brothers that I know of, now go get me another biscuit."

Jimmy came back out of the kitchen with the biscuit and said, "When my big brother comes back, he's going to take me away from here, and you'll all miss me, and then you'll be sorry."

Frank hollered, "Goddamn Vikings." So Jimmy went out in the alley and tried to pry a loose board off the back of Mrs. Payne's shed to make a skateboard with and he didn't think much else about his big brother.

But then one day soon after that it was Saturday and Frank and Carla drove out to the mall to pick up a couple of movies for the weekend.

Jimmy stayed home. He was in the driveway trying to make a rocket launcher out of a piece of pipe and the bottom half of a Clorox jug when a man on a motorcycle came up the street and stopped in front of the driveway.

The motorcycle was loud and shiny and blue. The man had long hair and a beard and heavy boots.

It was Jesus. Jesus Christ.

Jesus didn't have to say anything. Jimmy just put down his rocket launcher and climbed up on back of the motorcycle. They scratched off in the gravel and roared down the street. An empty Ho Ho's wrapper rose up out of the ditch and scooted along after them a few feet then coasted back down to the pavement.

They turned left heading west on old Winchester Pike disappearing into the sun on the horizon which was sliding down into the blue hills like the blade of a slow orange guillotine.

On their way to the mall Frank and Carla passed some cars along the side of the street that looked like they had been abandoned. Some still had their radios on.

And when they got to the mall the air conditioning had just then broken down so all the doors were propped open. There weren't many people shopping and all of the clerks were standing around in front of the stores looking up one way then down the other like something had just then happened and a hot dry wind whistled down the length of the concrete block arcade. . .

About the Author

Tony Crunk's first collection of poetry, *Living in the Resurrection*, was the 1994 selection in the Yale Series of Younger Poets. He has since published two other collections of poetry and three books for children. He lives in Birmingham, Alabama.

About the Artist

Peter Wilm is a musician and visual artist living in Birmingham, Alabama. He's been drawing little black and white pictures since he was kid.